# Fred and Finn

by Madeline Goodey

illustrated by Mike Gordon

READZ NE

# Fred and Finn

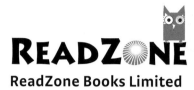

# READZNE
## Readzone Books Limited

First published in this edition 2015

© in this edition ReadZone Books Limited 2015
© in text Madeline Goodey 2009
© in illustrations Mike Gordon 2009

Madeline Goodey has asserted her right under the Copyright Designs and Patents Act 1988 to be identified as the author of this work.

Mike Gordon has asserted his right under the Copyright Designs and Patents Act 1988 to be identified as the illustrator of this work.

Every attempt has been made by the Publisher to secure appropriate permissions for material reproduced in this book. If there has been any oversight we will be happy to rectify the situation in future editions or reprints. Written submissions should be made to the Publisher.

British Library Cataloguing in Publication Data (CIP) is available for this title.

Printed in Malta by Melita Press.

ISBN 978 1 78322 411 1

Visit our website: www.readzonebooks.com

Fat frog Finn and
thin frog Fred
were jumping up
and down.

Along came a fly.

Up jumped fat Finn and grabbed
that tasty fly!

8

Thin Fred was too slow.

10

Along came a slippery slug.

12

Down jumped fat Finn and… …

gobbled up that slippery slug.

Thin frog Fred was too slow, again.

17

Along came a
lovely bug.

Under the branch
jumped fat frog Finn…

21

...and got stuck!
He couldn't move.

Thin frog Fred jumped over the branch and ate that lovely bug. At last!

Fat frog Finn could not move.

Thin frog Fred munched
on a juicy caterpillar.

Fat frog Finn still could not
move.

Thin frog
Fred had a
berry for his
pudding.

So fat frog Finn got thin and thin frog Fred got fat!

# Did you enjoy this book?

Look out for more *Magpies* titles –
fun stories in 150 words

**The Clumsy Cow** by Julia Moffat and Lisa Williams
ISBN 978 1 78322 157 8

**The Disappearing Cheese** by Paul Harrison and Ruth Rivers
ISBN 978 1 78322 470 8

**Flying South** by Alan Durant and Kath Lucas
ISBN 978 1 78322 410 4

**Fred and Finn** by Madeline Goodey and Mike Gordon
ISBN 978 1 78322 411 1

**Growl!** by Vivian French and Tim Archbold
ISBN 978 1 78322 412 8

**I Wish I Was an Alien** by Vivian French and Lisa Williams
ISBN 978 1 78322 413 5

**Lovely, Lovely Pirate Gold** by Scoular Anderson
ISBN 978 1 78322 206 3

**Pet to School Day** by Hilary Robinson and Tim Archbold
ISBN 978 1 78322 471 5

**Tall Tilly** by Jillian Powell and Tim Archbold
ISBN 978 1 78322 414 2

**Terry the Flying Turtle** by Anna Wilson and Mike Gordon
ISBN 978 1 78322 415 9

**Too Small** by Kay Woodward and Deborah van de Leijgraaf
ISBN 978 1 78322 156 1

**Turn Off the Telly** by Charlie Gardner and Barbara Nascimbeni
ISBN 978 1 78322 158 5